# My Secret World

## Mystical Mermaids

Kay Woodward

Illustrated by Strawberrie Donnelly

**PUFFIN**

PUFFIN BOOKS

Published by the Penguin Group
Penguin Books Ltd, 80 Strand, London WC2R 0RL, England
Penguin Group (USA) Inc., 375 Hudson Street, New York, New York 10014, USA
Penguin Group (Canada), 90 Eglinton Avenue East, Suite 700, Toronto, Ontario, Canada
M4P 2Y3 (a division of Pearson Penguin Canada Inc.)
Penguin Ireland, 25 St Stephen's Green, Dublin 2, Ireland (a division of Penguin Books Ltd)
Penguin Group (Australia), 250 Camberwell Road, Camberwell, Victoria 3124, Australia
(a division of Pearson Australia Group Pty Ltd)
Penguin Books India Pvt Ltd, 11 Community Centre, Panchsheel Park,
New Delhi – 110 017, India
Penguin Group (NZ), cnr Airborne and Rosedale Roads, Albany, Auckland 1310,
New Zealand (a division of Pearson New Zealand Ltd)
Penguin Books (South Africa) (Pty) Ltd, 24 Sturdee Avenue, Rosebank, Johannesburg 2196,
South Africa

Penguin Books Ltd, Registered Offices: 80 Strand, London WC2R 0RL, England

penguin.com

Published 2006
1

Text copyright © Kay Woodward, 2006
Illustrations copyright © Strawberrie Donnelly, 2006
All rights reserved

The moral right of the author and illustrator has been asserted

Set in Weiss
Made and printed in England by Clays Ltd, St Ives plc

British Library Cataloguing in Publication Data
A CIP catalogue record for this book is available from the British Library

ISBN-13: 978–0–141–33085–4
ISBN-10: 0–141–32085–0

# Contents

# Welcome to the secret world of mermaids . . .

*H*ave you ever been lucky enough to see a real mermaid? Have you ever caught sight of one of these secretive creatures combing their long, glossy hair or plunging into the deepest part of the ocean to search for pretty shells?

If you've never seen a mermaid, you're not alone. Mermaids are very shy. These mystical beings prefer to stay out of the limelight — instead, they spend their time singing, swimming or getting to know the wonderful sea creatures that live with them deep beneath the sea.

How much do you really know about mermaids?

Why are their tails so glittery? How do they learn how to swim? What language do they speak? And where do baby mermaids sleep? Take a deep breath and dive into the secret world of mermaids to find out the answers to these important questions and more besides . . .

## Chapter One
## All about mermaids

*T*he seawater is so calm that it seems like a sheet
of turquoise glass. Then a tiny ripple rolls
outwards – a circle that grows wider and wider
before vanishing. Suddenly . . . splash! A creature
breaks the surface, and water streams down a sleek,
golden head. This may look just like a young girl, but
it is actually a true, real-life mermaid.

Mermaids live in the world's seas and oceans,
and while many people have searched for the
tiniest glimpse of a golden tail or shining hair,
even more have failed. Just a lucky few have

managed to spot these wonderful creatures —
and that's how we know about them.

## Location, location, location

Mermaids live in saltwater seas and oceans all
around the world – from chilly Antarctica to
the sizzling Caribbean. Wherever there are
rocks and sea, you'll find mermaids – if you look
hard enough. Although they love to glide
through water with their fishy friends, they

never stray too far from dry land where they
can rest. But they stay away from busy seaside

resorts, preferring quiet, secluded places, where they are less likely to be spotted by curious onlookers.

Under the sea, there's a whole mermaid world for these wonderful creatures to enjoy. The seabed is one giant playground, while caves are cosy undersea rooms. You may wonder why they choose to spend time perched on boring old rocks – but to a mermaid a sharp rock is a gorgeous silken couch, where she can relax and watch the world go by.

## Part-human, part-fish

From the waist up, a mermaid looks like a human. But that's where the similarity ends, because instead of two legs she has a beautiful long tail. Mermaids can enjoy the best of both worlds. They can dive to the bottom of the ocean to collect seashells, then shoot back to the surface and wriggle on to a rock to breathe fresh air.

Of all sea creatures, mermaids are probably the most intelligent – they're even cleverer than dolphins! This is one of the reasons they like to spend so much time sitting in the sun. This valuable thinking time is when they come up with their best ideas.

## A mermaid's heart

Mermaids do not fall in love easily – they are actually quite fussy. But, once a mermaid does fall in love, she falls in love forever. Even if they live apart, she will remain totally loyal to her true love until the day she dies.

Strangely, mermaids do not often fall for mermen – male mermaids. (A merman has the upper body of a man and the tail of a fish.) They prefer real men, especially seafaring fellows who sail the high seas for a living. Of all men, sailors know the most about the mermaids' world. They love the feeling of salty spray on skin and the sea breeze as it ruffles their hair.

This shared love of
the sea means that
mermaids and sailors
get on tremendously
well.

## Mystical mermaid facts

✫ In French, 'la mer' means 'sea'. So, the word 'mermaid' means 'maid of the sea'.

✫ Mermaids have lungs, like humans, which allow them to breathe air, but they also have heart-shaped gills behind their ears, so they can breathe underwater too, like fish.

✫ Never disturb a mermaid when she is daydreaming or thinking deeply. Although she may look awake, her whole mind will be in dream mode. You could give her a terrible fright!

## Chapter Two
## Little mermaids

The baby mermaid's eyelids flutter open, and she gazes around with deep blue eyes. She is nestled in a cosy rock pool, wrapped in a thick layer of warm, wet seaweed. Spotting a rattle made of pink seashells, she gurgles with delight and makes a grab for it, shaking it madly. Clickety-click, clickety-clack! A beautiful face leans towards her, golden curls tickling the baby mermaid's face. The baby coos contentedly. Her mother is watching over her – she's safe.

When they are born, baby mermaids look just the same as grown-up mermaids, but they are much smaller – no bigger than a human baby.

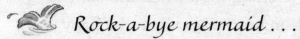 *Rock-a-bye mermaid . . .*

Instead of sleeping in a cradle or a cot, little merbabies snooze in shallow rock pools that are just big enough to hold them.

Here, their delicate tails are kept underwater so they won't dry out. Seaweed protects their tiny bodies from wind, rain and sun.

A newborn merbaby will spend half the day awake and half asleep. The merbaby's mother makes sure that the baby is watched over at all times (when she is busy, the seals will pitch

in to help), fetching food when the baby is hungry, and singing songs when the baby is tired. When accompanied by the gentle swooshing of the waves, a mermaid lullaby is guaranteed to send any merbaby to sleep.

Here is one popular lullaby
for baby mermaids . . .

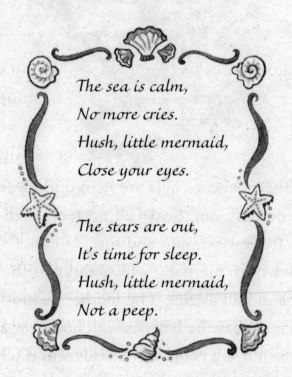

*The sea is calm,*
*No more cries.*
*Hush, little mermaid,*
*Close your eyes.*

*The stars are out,*
*It's time for sleep.*
*Hush, little mermaid,*
*Not a peep.*

 *Splash!*

Mermaids can swim long before they can speak.
As soon as a baby mermaid is able to sit upright
in her rock-pool cradle, her mother will gently
scoop the little one up and place her in the sea.

To begin with, the water is quite a shock –
the little mermaid is used to the rock pool,
which is warmed by the sun. Breathing lessons
can be a little tricky too – this will be the first
time the mermaid has used her gills. But, soon,
the lapping waves and the gentle sway of the
sea work their magic. With a flick of her tail,

the little mermaid dives beneath the surface and begins to explore the wonderful underwater world that awaits her . . .

## Lessons of the sea

You might think that mermaids don't have to go to school because there are no classrooms underwater – but you'd be wrong! Even though there are no brick walls, desks or chairs, mermaids do go to lessons. Shoals of friendly sea creatures tell the young mermaids all they need to know about the sea. For example, walruses are especially good at geography, while dolphins are expert aerobics instructors. Sharks teach survival skills, while one of the older mermaids usually takes singing lessons.

## Mystical mermaid facts

☆ When a mermaid is born, her tail is silvery. After a few years, it will turn golden. Then, after a few more years, it will gain a greenish shimmer because of the minerals in seawater.

☆ Seals make excellent babysitters. They are quite happy to sit beside a baby mermaid for hours, making sure that she comes to no harm. If the little one wakes, the seal will soothe her with a special barking sound.

☆ Unlike mermaids, humans need swimming lessons to teach us how to swim. But, once we learn, it is something that we will never forget.

## Chapter Three
## Beneath the waves

*T*hree mermaids bob about on the surface of the
sea, waiting patiently for the signal. A fourth
mermaid puts a conch shell to her lips and blows. Toot!
They're off! The mermaids turn tail and dive beneath
the water, hurtling down, down, down. As they swim,
the water grows darker, changing from blue to deepest
indigo. Suddenly, their eager fingers reach the seabed
– the halfway mark. With a whoosh, they race back
towards the surface.

If there were an underwater Olympics, mermaids
would win every single event. Beneath the

waves, no one can beat them for speed and agility.

## A fishy tail

By sunlight or moonlight – and even on the cloudiest day – a mermaid's tail is a wonderful thing. Its glittering and shimmering can be seen from far away, but it isn't until you take a closer look that you see how truly beautiful it is.

Just like a fish's, a mermaid's tail is covered in shiny scales. These over-lap slightly to allow the mermaid to wiggle her tail. The scales are made of bone, which is covered in a type of protective enamel. So, unlike human skin, a mermaid's tail is very

tough and durable. She can sit on the sharpest of rocks without coming to harm.

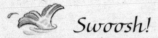 *Swoosh!*

Mermaids' tails are very flexible and powerful — this is why they are such talented swimmers. A mermaid swims by moving her tail up and down, rippling her whole body as she does so. You might be surprised to learn that humans can swim like mermaids too . . .

Most human divers wear a rubber fin on each foot, scissoring their legs as they swim. But a few divers swim just like mermaids. They put both of their feet into a single large fin, then wiggle their whole body to move through the water. It can be very tiring, but with a bit of practice and a lot of effort, monofin divers can speed through the water faster than their two-finned friends!

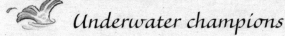

## Underwater champions

Mermaids are ultra competitive – they just love to win! So, at the Annual Underwater Championships (usually held in the last week of June and first week of July) there is no shortage of entrants for the different events. The proud winners are each presented with a shell pendant strung on to a garland of plaited seaweed.

## Round-the-rock relay

This is a traditional relay race with a difference – it's underwater! Instead of a metal baton, mermaids pass a piece of driftwood from one team member to another as they swim laps round a group of jagged rocks.

### Synchronized swimming

This is a very popular event. Teams of at least
two and sometimes as many as twenty mermaids
dive, somersault and pirouette under the water –
perfectly in time. And because they can breathe
underwater, they don't have to pinch their noses
closed with plastic pegs!

### The high jump

Originally invented by dolphins, this event is
becoming increasingly popular amongst the

mermaid community. Mermaids take turns to swim down to the seabed, before zooming upwards, breaking through the surface and shooting high into the air. If you ever see a school of dolphins leaping above the waves, look closely . . . Are they really dolphins or could they have been mermaids practising their leaps?

## Mystical mermaid facts

⭐ *A mermaid's tail fin contains fragments of pure gold — this is why it glitters so brightly.*

⭐ *The two special pointy fins at the end of a mermaid's tail are called flukes. When the mermaid moves her tail up and down, the flukes propel her through the water.*

⭐ *A mermaid can swim faster than a speedboat. So, if you happen to spot a mermaid while you're zooming about on the waves, there's no point chasing her. You'll never catch up.*

## Chapter Four
### When mermaids come to shore

The mermaid raises her head from the water and shades her eyes against the glare of the sun. From here, the shoreline is a long blurred strip of greeny-grey. She knows that as she swims closer, everything will become clearer, more solid, more real. Beaches and piers, harbours and marinas . . . She takes a deep, steadying breath. She must go on. For how else will she reach her true love?

Every once in a while, mermaids venture on to dry land and mingle with humans. Some may be curious and others just fancy a change from

bobbing about in the sea. The most common reason for shore leave is because they have fallen in love with a sailor . . .

## A magical transformation

If mermaids came ashore without disguising themselves, their photos would be plastered over the newspapers by the very next day. They'd be the top story on the one o'clock, six o'clock and the ten o'clock news. They would probably be starring in their own reality TV show by the end of the week. The poor mermaids wouldn't get a moment's peace. So this is why they change their form.

Before coming ashore, a mermaid performs a very special – and very magical – ceremony. She carefully wraps seaweed round and round herself, from her waist down to the tip of her tail. Then she closes her eyes, crosses her arms and murmurs a top-secret incantation. (Be sure not to repeat it to anyone!)

*Clad in seaweed, arms crossed tight,*
*Wish, wish, wish with all my might,*
*Grant this wish, O Neptune, do,*
*Make my tail become legs two!*

In a twinkling, the mermaid's tail transforms to become two long human legs. The seaweed changes into a long, flowing, emerald-green skirt, while a floaty white shirt covers the mermaid's bare shoulders. Hey presto! She is now beautifully disguised and ready to disappear into a crowd of people. No one will suspect a thing!

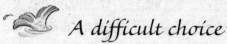 *A difficult choice*

It's not unheard of for a mermaid to fall in love with a man and stay on land forever, but it is very rare. The lure of the sea is very strong indeed. Even the most besotted mermaid may find herself running away from her true love and diving back into the welcoming waves. The few mermaids who live on land usually have their own indoor pools filled with salty water. Whenever they feel the urge to return to the sea, they plunge into the water instead and regain their fishy form for an hour or two.

## Mystical mermaid facts

✮ *Mermaids can speak many languages. They speak Mermish to each other, but they also know how to speak to dolphins (with clicks and whistles) and seals (with high- and low-pitched barks). They can speak to humans too — they learn the language of whichever country is nearest to their watery home.*

*When a mermaid is on land, she must be very careful not to get her legs wet – if this happens, they will instantly turn back into a fishy tail! And if you've ever watched a seal move on land, you'll understand how hard it would be for a mermaid to keep her tail on land.*

*Mermaids worship the legendary sea god, Neptune, who is said to rule the underwater world. He rides on the back of a dolphin and clasps a three-pronged spear called a trident.*

## Chapter Five
## Legendary mermaids

The girl paddles out of the sea and plods up the golden sand. She wishes for the millionth time that she could be a mermaid – free to explore the sea and make friends with starfish. It would be so wonderful. She reaches her family's beach umbrella and plonks herself beside her mum. And then she sees it – her well-thumbed book of mermaid legends! If she can't be a mermaid, she'll read about them instead . . .

Where the sea meets land, stories are often told of beautiful mermaids. Some of these mysterious and marvellous legends date back thousands of

years, while others are much newer, but all are utterly captivating.

## The mermaid of Zennor

The tiny Cornish village of Zennor is built on high, rocky cliffs overlooking the sea. It is said that here, long ago, a mermaid named Morveren ventured ashore to listen to the deep, tuneful voice of Matthew — a singer in the church choir. But Morveren's father had stern words for his daughter. She must stay well hidden at all times for, if people spotted her, she would be held prisoner on land. So, every evening, the mermaid would make her way up the steep hill to watch Matthew sing, always keeping well out of sight. And, every evening, she fell more and more deeply in love with him.

Soon, Morveren could resist the enchanting singing no longer and stepped from the shadows where she hid. Matthew saw her and chased after her — and so did the curious

villagers! Captivated by the mermaid's beauty, Matthew scooped Morveren into his arms and ran into the sea with her, leaving all his friends and family. They were never seen again.

Some say that Matthew's voice can still be heard from the depths of the sea, warning sailors of bad weather and treacherous seas. And, if you look closely inside the now-ruined church where Matthew once sang, you will see a mermaid's image carved on to an ancient bench.

## Melusina's secret

Many years ago, Count Siegfried ruled the tiny country of Luxembourg. According to legend, he met the charming and very pretty Melusina and asked her to marry him. Melusina had one

request. She wished to stay on her own for one
night and one day every month. No one should
spy on her. Of course, Siegfried agreed. He just
wanted to marry her – he would have given his
bride the moon if she'd asked for it.

But, as the years passed, the Count became
more and more curious. And, one night, he
crept to the door of his wife's secret chamber
and peeked inside. She was relaxing in a
frothy bubble bath. Count Siegfried frowned.
What was so secret about that? Then he spotted
the long, silvery tail hanging over the side of

the bath . . . Melusina's head whirled round immediately. She gave the Count a look of disappointment and, without a word, dived from the bathroom window into the River Alzette. She never came back.

## Mystical mermaid facts

☆ Mermaids can see, hear, touch, smell and taste really well. But did you know that they have a magical sixth sense too? This sense allows mermaids to know when they are being watched, talked about or even if someone is thinking of them. It also warns when danger is approaching . . .

☆ For every mermaid that is spotted, another million remain hidden below the waves.

☆ A Japanese legend says that mermaids do not cry wet, salty tears like us. Instead, they cry real pearls.

## Chapter Six
## Mystical sea creatures

*T*he girl peers over the side of the speedboat and
*give*s a cry of recognition. Mermaids! She can
see a whole crowd of them below, swimming up
through the seawater towards her. They pop their
heads above the surf and come closer and closer. And
then the girl's heart sinks. These are not mermaids –
they are dolphins . . . Then she grins, because dolphins
are truly beautiful creatures too.

Although many people believe that mermaids
really exist, some people are uncertain. They
think that in the past people may have spotted

other sea creatures and mistaken them for mermaids . . .

 *I spy with my little eye . . .*
Christopher Columbus was a famous navigator who sailed across the Atlantic in 1492 and discovered America, then called the 'New World'. The next year, he and his crew were bobbing around in the sea near Haiti in the Caribbean. Columbus noted in his diary that one of his crewmen had seen three mermaids near Haiti. However, he also wrote that the mermaids weren't terribly pretty, leading many to believe that his fellow sailor may actually have seen three seals.

 *Sea cows*

Dugongs are large sea creatures with two front flippers and dolphin-like tails. They have smooth, grey-brown skin and fine hair. Dugongs are sometimes called 'sea cows', because they like to graze on sea grasses.

They measure up to three metres in length and weigh as much as a cow too!

From far away, a dugong's face looks a little like a human face. But, if you want to see for yourself, the best place for dugong-spotting is

off the coast of Australia. If you're lucky enough to go there on holiday – or even live there! – then head for Shark Bay in Western Australia or Hervey Bay in Queensland, and keep your eyes peeled.

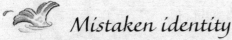

## Mistaken identity

Dolphins and mermaids are more than a little alike, so it's no wonder that they've been mistaken for each other. They both have long, bendy tails. They both have twin tail flukes – the fins at the end of the tail – to help speed them through the water. And when the sun reflects off the dolphin's wet head or the mermaid's wet hair, they both look very glossy.

Marine experts think that, in the past, many supposed 'mermaid' sightings have actually been glimpses of dolphins. But there's one thing these experts haven't considered . . . How many times have people seen 'dolphins' in the distance, when these have actually been mermaids . . .?

## ✵ Mystical mermaid facts

Acetabularia is a type of plant found in warm seas. It is sometimes called mermaid's wineglass, because of the tiny cup that grows at the end of each slender stalk. You never know, if you ever find the plant, you might catch sight of a mermaid drinking from it . . .

✿ Esther Williams starred in lots of films during the 1940s and 1950s. But she wasn't an actress — she was a swimmer! Esther became known as Hollywood's mermaid, because of her amazing watery moves.

✿ Water-silk grows in fresh water. When the beautiful, thin strands float to the surface, they look just like long hair. The plant is also known as mermaid tresses, because it can so easily be mistaken for mermaids' hair.

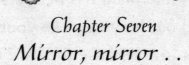

## Chapter Seven
### *Mirror, mirror . . .*

*S*hafts of bright sunlight pierce the turquoise water, making the mermaid's world sparkle and glow. She grins delightedly and, with a wiggle of her powerful tail, shoots to the surface. Gracefully, the mermaid slithers on to a large outcrop, waiting as the sun warms her body. She peeps inside the rocky crevice where she keeps her box of treasures. It's about time for some beauty treatments!

Mermaids live a very long time – sometimes well over 250 years. So how do they all stay

looking so young and so lovely? Read on to
find out what mermaids do to keep themselves
looking tippity-top . . .

### A dazzling reflection . . .

Each and every mermaid has her very own shell
mirror (to find out how to make yours, turn to
page 52). This isn't because they are terribly
vain – they just like to make sure that they look
good. After all, there are no bathroom mirrors
at sea, and the water's surface doesn't always
stay smooth enough to reflect a mermaid's face.

It's quite common for
mermaids' mirrors to
speak back to their
owners (this only
works if you're a
mermaid – sorry!).
They offer critical
advice, such as . . .

You've got
seaweed caught
in your hair!

You might want to wash behind those ears!

Would you look at the state of your nails!

. . . but they say lovely things too!

## . . . *from head* . . .

All mermaids have beautiful long hair. Sometimes it's curly, sometimes it's straight, but it's always long. (Well, have you ever seen an underwater hairdresser?) Unfortunately, the sea can play havoc with hair, making it salty and brittle. So mermaids spend a lot of time making sure that their lovely locks stay in good condition. Once a week, they dribble cod-liver oil over their hair – this keeps it thick and healthy. A quick rinse

with a mixture of lemon juice and water adds a super shine. Mermaids take great care to keep the cod-liver oil and lemon juice out of their eyes – otherwise, it can really sting.

Mermaids have no need for hairdryers – their tresses get soaking wet every time they go swimming – but to avoid knots and tangles, they use a special comb made of coral. It takes at least a hundred strokes with a comb to make sure their hair is perfectly groomed.

 . . . *to tail*

A mermaid's tail sparkles and shimmers so brightly because she polishes it with a sponge three times a week. She also looks out for limpets, barnacles and other types of clingy sea creatures – these often attach themselves to her

tail as she swims
past. But the
mermaid doesn't
pick off the shellfish
– she whispers softly
to them in their own
language. The sound of her
voice is so soothing that the creatures
voluntarily unstick themselves and hang on to
nearby rocks instead. Sometimes, if she's in a
rush, a mermaid might employ a friendly fish
to help her tidy up her tail . . .

## Mystical mermaid facts

☆ *Did you know that mermaids do not use
any make-up at all? They have long,
naturally curly eyelashes. Their cheeks glow with the
effort of swimming. And the water that glistens on
their faces is sparklier than any glitter!*

☆ Mermaids keep their elbows silky smooth by rubbing them morning and night with handfuls of gritty sand.

☆ One of the biggest reasons why mermaids look so young is because they smile so much. It has been scientifically proven that a happy mermaid looks about fifty years younger than a miserable one.

## Chapter Eight
### Mermaid-spotting

*T*he girl shields her eyes from the bright sun and peers into the distance. She can see a rocky outcrop at the far end of the bay. Perched on the highest rock, she's really, nearly, almost sure that she can see a mermaid, especially if she squints. The magical creature is holding a mirror and combing her long hair. Donk! A beachball bounces off the girl's head and she looks crossly at her brother. When she looks back at the rock, the mermaid is gone . . .

Mermaid-spotting is notoriously difficult, but, armed with a little expert knowledge, you might

increase your chances of seeing one of these beautiful creatures for yourself.

*Top five tips for mermaid-spotting*

Gathered from the world's greatest mermaid-spotters, these tips might help you in your quest . . .

1. **Be alert** – if you're near the coast, you could spot a mermaid at any time. So, make sure you're ready!

2. **Keep watch on land and sea** – seashores are the number-one spot for seeing mermaids, but you might see them on boat trips too. Watch the waves for any sign of a glossy head or shiny tail.

3. **Wear sunglasses** – mermaids are very sparkly creatures, so sparkly that they can dazzle you with their brightness. By wearing sunglasses you'll cut out the glare and be able to see them properly.

4. **Keep your distance** – if you do see a mermaid, it's vital that you don't get too near. You might frighten her off before you've had a chance to look at her properly.

5. **Never look away** – the moment you blink or look away from a mermaid is the moment she will disappear.

 *Make-believe mermaids*

If you're not lucky enough to spot mermaids in real life, don't despair! You can always find them in books, at the cinema and on television too. *The Little Mermaid* is a famous tale by Hans Christian Andersen – one of the world's greatest storytellers. It tells of a beautiful young mermaid with a wonderful singing voice who falls in love with a human prince and then . . . Sorry! There's no space to tell you what happens here – and it would spoil the ending. To find out what happens, you'll have to read the story yourself!

You might have seen the famous Disney film of *The Little Mermaid* (1989), which won two Oscars. But did you know that it has a different ending to Hans Christian Andersen's original story? Why not read the book and watch the film to decide which ending you like best? *Splash* (1984) is a classic movie about a mermaid who falls in love with a man (this happens quite a lot in mermaid stories). It's quite an old film – starring Daryl Hannah and Tom Hanks – but you might be able to get hold of a copy on DVD.

## Mystical mermaid facts

☆ *In the sixteenth century, top playwright William Shakespeare wrote about mermaids in* A Midsummer Night's Dream. *Oberon, who is king of the fairies, says that a mermaid's singing is so charming that it calms rough seas and makes stars shoot through the sky.*

☆ A merrow is an Irish mermaid, but instead of a tail she has webbed hands and feet. Legend says that when a merrow is seen, stormy weather is on its way.

☆ If you ever visit Copenhagan in Denmark, look out for the statue of Hans Christian Andersen's Little Mermaid. It stands at the harbour to remind everyone what a good storyteller he was!

## Chapter Nine
## Mermaid magic

There's an enchanting melody weaving its way across the sea. It is as sweet as honey and as soft as velvet. All who hear the tune fall under its spell. One sailor leans against the side of his boat, staring wistfully across the waves. He doesn't recognize the song and he doesn't know who sings it, but he does know that he has to find her. The sailor drags his attention back to the boat, unfurls a sail and spins the wheel. Then he speeds towards the music.

According to legend, a mermaid can lure a sailor across the sea with the power of her voice alone.

But how can you talk with mermaids? Here are just a few magical ways to get in touch . . .

## A magical mermaid pool

Trudging across endless sandy beaches in search of mermaids is time consuming and very tiring. There's no guarantee that you'll find a mermaid obediently perched on a rock, just waiting to be discovered, but don't despair. There is another way to get close to these elusive creatures.

1. Find a big bowl or a sink – it's best if this is in a quiet place, where nosy brothers and sisters won't disturb you.

2. Gather together any or all of the following – pebbles, seashells, glitter, petals and leaves.

3. Half-fill your bowl or sink with water. If you have a bottle of blue food colouring handy, add just one or two drops to the water and swirl it around. It'll look just like the sea!

4. Carefully place the pebbles and seashells in

the water, then sprinkle the glitter, petals and leaves over the surface.

5. Half-close your eyes and gaze at the pretty, sparkling pool you've created. Now, place your fingertips in the water, think pure mermaid thoughts and imagine what it must be like to speak to mermaids. What would you ask? What would they reply? You never know, your answers might come direct from the ocean . . .

## A magical voice

One of the easiest – and loveliest – ways to get in touch with mermaids is by singing to them. Mermaids love music just as much as they love the sea. They don't just sing haunting melodies to sailors, they entertain each other with sea shanties and practise musical scales while they

are combing their hair. In fact, you can pretty much guarantee that whenever a mermaid's head is above water, she will be singing.

Do you love to sing? Try humming along to your favourite pop songs – you could learn the words too. Imagine that your singing can be heard in the ocean . . . And if your school has a choir, why not join? After all, there's only one thing better than a mermaid singing – and that's lots of mermaids singing!

## Mystical mermaid facts

☆ To a mermaid, there's nothing worse than a cold — it's very bad for the voice. So, to keep her voice silky smooth and totally tuneful, a mermaid brews herself a special drink before bedtime. A seashell filled with warm water, a squirt of lemon juice and a dollop of honey is the best way to ward off a sniffly nose and croaky throat.

☆ When mermaids come to shore — whether they have fallen in love or if they are just curious — they bring large seashells with them. Whenever they feel homesick, they lift the shell to their ear and listen to the sound of the sea. Try it — it works!

☆ It is rumoured that mermaids belong to the world of fairies. Experts are searching round the clock for evidence that these beautiful fishy creatures are really magical too.

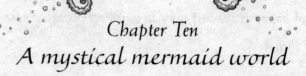

## Chapter Ten
## A mystical mermaid world

*I*f you love mermaids, why not create your very own mermaid treasures? Then, whenever you like, you can dive into your very own mermaid world!

### A mermaid mirror

A seashell mirror is part of the essential mermaid kit. But you don't have to hunt out a mermaid shop or go to the beach to find one – it's quite easy to make your own! You'll need:

- ✵ Tracing paper
- ✵ A pencil
- ✵ Card
- ✵ A pair of scissors
- ✵ A piece of foil
- ✵ A stapler
- ✵ Sticky tape
- ✵ Shell-shaped pasta (called conchiglie)
- ✵ Glue
- ✵ Paint
- ✵ A paintbrush
- ✵ A glitter pen

1. First, make a card mirror following the outline on the next page. Trace the image on to tracing paper and flip the paper over. Then, pressing firmly with a pencil, rub this outline on to a piece of card. Or, if you're feeling more artistic, copy the mirror outline straight on to the card. Cut out the mirror shape.

2. Make a second mirror shape in exactly the same way.

3. Lay a piece of foil over the mirror shape, with the shiny side facing upwards. Carefully smooth the foil over the card and tuck all of the edges underneath until the entire piece of card

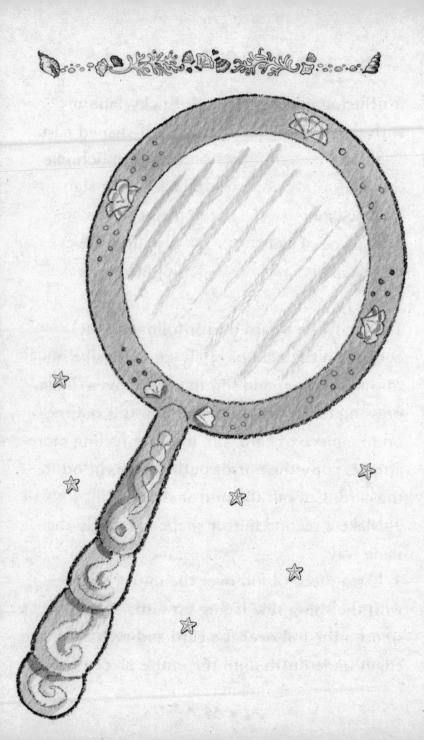

is neatly covered in shiny foil. Do the same with the second mirror shape.

4. Staple the two pieces of card together, so that the untidy edges of foil are out of sight, sandwiched between the two cards. Pop an extra staple through the handle. Cover the backs of the staples with sticky tape to make sure there are no sharp edges.

5. Decorate your pasta shapes with paint (you must ask a grown-up to help you do this – it can get quite messy) or with a glitter pen. Or you could simply leave the pasta plain, which looks very stylish too!

6. Using pieces of rolled-up sticky tape or dabs of glue, stick the pasta shells around the edge of the mirror.

You're done! Now, all you need to do is comb your hair while you gaze into your terrific mermaid mirror!

## A mermaid charm necklace

Mermaids can't resist jewellery, especially charm necklaces. They like to hang their favourite trinkets and keepsakes on them, to remind them of how much they love the sea. Here's what you need to make your own charm necklace:

- ✭ A piece of strong silvery or golden thread
- ✭ Tracing paper
- ✭ A pencil

- ✭ Card
- ✭ Scissors
- ✭ Felt-tip pens or pencils
- ✭ A glitter pen

1. In the same way that you made the card mirror (see page 52), follow the outlines on the next page to make seashell, starfish, mermaid and moon charms for your necklace. Trace or copy the shapes and cut them out. Colour the charms with felt-tips or coloured pencils – the brighter the better! You could also decorate

them with a glitter pen to make them really eye
catching. Remember to colour and decorate
both sides of the charms in case they flip over
while you're wearing the necklace.

2. Ask an adult to make a hole at the top of
each charm.

3. Thread the first charm on to the thread, then tie a knot to keep it in position. One at a time, thread on the remaining charms, tying each one as you go.

Then all you need to do is tie your necklace in a bow at the back of your neck and wear your mermaid charms with pride!

## A mermaid sleeping bag

Why not transform a boring sleeping bag into your own swishy mermaid's tail? It's perfect for a mermaid sleepover! Here's what you'll need:

☆ An old sleeping bag
☆ A piece of curtain netting or silky material

☆ One metre of thin rope
☆ A needle and thread
☆ Stick-on sequins

1. Before you start, make sure your sleeping bag is an old one that no one wants and not a super-duper Arctic-strength bag that your big sister or brother is planning on taking on an extreme camping trip. If it's old and tatty and no one wants it? Fantastic!

2. Tie the rope around the bottom of the sleeping bag, about 20 cm from the end. The sleeping bag will now narrow to a point at the end, forming the end of the tail.

3. Decorate the netting. Go really wild and stick the sequins all over it, to make the netting ultra sparkly. There is no such thing as 'too many sparkles'.

4. Carefully tuck the netting into the rope, bunching it up as you go, so that it's gathered at the end of the sleeping bag and fans out wonderfully.

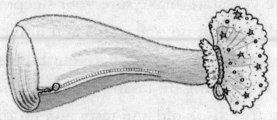

5. Ask your mum or dad to sew the netting in place. A row of stitches just below the rope will secure both layers of netting.

Every time you slip inside your special sleeping bag you'll look like a mermaid, especially if you wiggle your legs. Better still, when you go to sleep, you'll drift away on a sea of mermaid dreams to enjoy your very own mermaid adventures . . .